TO & FRO

FAST & SLOW

DURGA BERNHARD

WALKER & COMPANY

NEW YORK

This book is dedicated to

all children who live in two worlds—

especially my own two beloveds:

Jonah and Eve

First published in the United States of America in 2001 by
Walker Publishing Company, Inc.

Published simultaneously in Canada by Fitzhenry and Whiteside, Markham, Ontario L3R 4T8

Library of Congress Cataloging-in-Publication Data
Bernhard, Durga
To & fro, fast & slow / Durga Bernhard.
p. m.
Summary: A girl who is shuttled between the homes of her divorced parents observes such opposites as "over, under," "rainy, sunny," and "full & empty."
ISBN 0-8027-8782-7 — ISBN 0-8027-8783-5
[1. English language—Synonyms and antonyms—Fiction. 2. Divorce—Fiction.] I. Title: To and fro, fast and slow. II. Title.
PZ7.B45517 To 2001
[E]—dc21

2001017874

Book design by Durga Bernhard
Typographical design and book composition by Diane Hobbing of Snap-Haus Graphics

Printed in Hong Kong

2 4 6 8 10 9 7 5 3 1

south

& north

back &

forth

over

under

work

& play

rainy

sad & funny

in & out

night

& day

to & fro

fast &

slow

full & empty

warm

& cold

new
&
old

noisy